Witter, Evelyn
Claw foot

claw foot

claw foot

by evelyn witter

illustrated by
sandra heinen

lerner publications company
minneapolis, minnesota

To my husband, William W. Witter, without whose love and encouragement this book could not have been written

LIBRARY OF CONGRESS CATALOGING IN PUBLICATION DATA

Witter, Evelyn.
Claw Foot.

SUMMARY: By learning to use his talents instead of dwelling on his handicap, Claw Foot, a lame Sioux Indian boy, earns a new name for himself.

[1. Indians of North America—Fiction. 2. Physically handicapped—Fiction] I. Heinen, Sandra, ill. II. Title.

PZ7.W78434Cl   [Fic]   74-33524
ISBN 0-8225-0641-6

Published simultaneously in Canada by J. M. Dent & Sons (Canada) Ltd., Don Mills, Ontario.

Manufactured in the United States of America

International Standard Book Number: 0-8225-0641-6
Library of Congress Catalog Card Number: 74-33524

CONTENTS

1 Arrow Through the Hoop   7

2 Horses Coming   14

3 Shadow   23

4 To Ride a Horse   31

5 The Search   40

6 An Unexpected Meeting   50

7 Broken Wing   57

1
ARROW THROUGH THE HOOP

Claw Foot stood at the open flap of the tepee. He could hear the voices of the other boys down by the river. He knew he must join them, or his mother, Falling Star, would call him back into the tepee to help her.

Woman's work was not for a boy! Not even a boy with a foot shaped like a claw.

Claw Foot looked down at his left foot. Even the carefully made doeskin moccasin could not disguise its gnarled, twisted shape.

"The only son of a great Sioux chief should be

7

strong and swift," thought Claw Foot bitterly. "Why was I, of all people, born with such a foot?"

Just then he heard his best friend, White Feather, call to him. "Come on!" White Feather shouted. "We are playing shoot-through-the-hoop."

Claw Foot stepped back into the tepee and reached for his quiver of blunt arrows and his bow, which were hanging from one of the tepee poles.

"I am glad you are joining the other boys." Falling Star smiled lovingly at him. But Claw Foot knew he could not win against boys who ran with strong, straight feet. Still, he must try. He must show courage. That was the Sioux way.

As Claw Foot limped toward the river, he noticed the sun sinking to the edge of the world, and he was glad. The games could not last long. Perhaps he could make a good showing in the short time before darkness came. There was always hope. But there was fear, too, and there was always the gnarled foot to stop him.

The games were already started when Claw Foot came close to the river's edge. He stood for a minute behind a clump of saplings as if to hide. He knew he would suffer humiliation, as always, and he was in no hurry to begin.

"Claw Foot!" called Red Duck, the most skillful and most disdainful of all the boys. "Come, crippled one. Try to take your place among us."

Claw Foot felt anger. He always felt anger when Red Duck spoke to him. It was not what Red Duck said that caused the anger to well up within Claw Foot. It was the scornful curl of his thin lips. It was the way he tossed his head to show how superior he was. It was the way he seemed to enjoy seeing a great chief's son limping on a gnarled, twisted, toes-bent foot.

Leaving the temporary seclusion of the saplings, Claw Foot edged nearer the line of boys. He saw Big Owl, the brave Sioux warrior whom he admired almost as much as his own father. Big Owl lined the boys up along the mark he had drawn with a willow twig. Then he took his place on the rise of ground that ran parallel to the river.

"Ohee!" Big Owl cried in his deep, melodious voice as he rolled the willow hoop. It was a strong hoop, one that Big Owl had made for the boys.

As the hoop rolled, the boys fired their blunt arrows through the circle. Those whose arrows went through the circle cried out with joy and made a mark on the ground to record the success.

Claw Foot stood straight. He drew back his bow-string and aimed carefully. The arrow whizzed easily through the circle, and his mark was made on the ground.

The sun was slowly edging away. Still, Claw Foot thought it would be some time before the sun was gone. The sun moved too slowly today.

Big Owl was moving farther up the rise and farther away from the boys.

"Now," he called to them through his cupped hands, "as the hoop rolls, run with it and shoot through the hoop as you run."

Claw Foot stiffened at the command. He would have liked to go back to the saplings and watch. But that was not the Sioux way. He must try.

He stood firmly and waited for Big Owl to start the hoop rolling down the hill. Perhaps this time he could fire an arrow through the hoop as he ran.

Red Duck turned to grin at him.

"Ohee!" he heard Big Owl call.

He saw the strong willow hoop start its descent. With all the force he could gather, Claw Foot ran, his bow held high in shooting position. Red Duck passed him. White Feather passed him. Other boys passed him. Claw Foot ran on.

He was gaining on the hoop, although his foot throbbed and his chest ached for air. He kept his eye on the rolling hoop. Then it hit a stump and teetered. When the hoop slowed, many of the boys got their shots through.

Claw Foot hurried. If the hoop dropped to the ground, the game was over, and he would have no chance to score. But the stump did not stop the hoop. It merely slowed it. "Now," thought Claw Foot, "I have a chance."

Running beside the hoop, he took aim. Suddenly he felt a sharp pain in his left foot as it bent over to the side. He felt himself falling and hitting the earth. His head struck a rock, and he seemed to be spinning in circles of red, yellow, and blue. His foot felt heavy with pain, and his head throbbed. Far away he heard the laughter of Red Duck.

"He was downed by a gopher hole!" laughed Red Duck. "The hoop almost stopped for him and still he could not shoot an arrow through it!" he shouted between gales of laughter.

"Anyone can trip in a gopher hole," he heard White Feather shout back.

Claw Foot closed his eyes. He lay against the earth, the mother of all. He took comfort in her

11

closeness. He wanted nothing more than to lie close to the earth in his misery. He could not run like the other boys. He could not even send a pointless arrow through a hoop that stood still for him. He was a claw foot who must bear the burden of shame all the days of his life. Why had the Great One chosen him to be so slow and useless?

As he lay there he heard the voices of the boys moving away. Then he felt a tap on his shoulder. He looked up to see White Feather.

"The sun is going down," White Feather said. "It is time to return to camp."

"I will not return," said Claw Foot. "Go on without me."

White Feather hesitated, reached out his hand as if to speak, then turned away and ran to catch up with the others.

Claw Foot laid his face against the earth. "I shall not be known as Claw Foot always," he said aloud. "I shall one day be known by another name . . . another name!"

At that moment he heard a deep, gentle voice above him.

"You can have a new name only if you earn one," Big Owl said.

Claw Foot turned to lie on his back, and he looked up into the handsome face of the warrior. He had not known that Big Owl could speak so gently.

"I cannot change my foot," he told the warrior.

"No. You cannot change your foot," Big Owl said, looking down at him. There was kindness in the big man's black eyes. "But you cannot let one foot be more important than the rest of your body. You must use what you have and not feel sorry for what you have not."

Then Big Owl moved away as silently as he had come.

Claw Foot felt a new excitement stirring deep inside of him. He wanted to talk to Big Owl again. Big Owl was wise and kind. Big Owl knew many things. Did he really think Claw Foot could earn a new name?

2
HORSES COMING

Rising, Claw Foot started to make his way back to the circle of tepees. He walked in the splendor of the setting sun, enjoying the gold and the crimson it cast on the land around him.

There was much beauty to see in this land of the Great One. A boy's feet could carry him far. But the feet of a horse could carry him farther.

Thoughts began racing over his mind like water over the rapids. A sure-footed horse could go over the land as fast as the wind. And all over the land there lay adventures and great deeds to do. From great deeds might come a new name.

A horse was the answer! But not one of his father's many horses. Not any of the horses on whom he had learned to ride and to shoot. He must have a horse of his own, who knew only his commands—no one else's. Together he and his horse would seek a great new name.

Tomorrow he would talk to Big Owl. He would ask Big Owl if it were true that a horse of his own would help him get a new name.

That night he dreamed of a horse. The horse he dreamed of was like a shadow. It had shape, but no color except for its feet. It had four white feet. They were strong feet, sure and solid in their step.

When morning came, Claw Foot rose. He dipped a bone spoon in the stewpot, ate quickly, and made his way to the tepee of Big Owl.

At Big Owl's tepee he lifted the flap. The warrior was sitting cross-legged on his bed robe. He motioned Claw Foot to sit opposite him.

"I want a horse of my own," Claw Foot blurted out. "One that I will train myself. A horse who will answer my commands. A horse who will know my thoughts as I will know his."

"Why do you want such a horse?" Big Owl asked, studying Claw Foot with his intense eyes.

15

"With such a horse I will have four good feet at my command. With four good feet I can travel far and do great deeds. Great deeds make a great name."

Claw Foot saw Big Owl's eyes light with approval.

"You have made a beginning," Big Owl said. "When you command the will of a good horse, you have power."

Again the excitement Claw Foot had felt the day before welled up within him. Big Owl was wise, and Big Owl agreed that a horse of his own was the beginning of a new name. Big Owl understood.

Then Big Owl's eyes looked deeply into his. "Have you seen a horse you would have for your own?" he asked.

"Only in a dream," Claw Foot confided. "In my dream I saw a horse with four white feet."

Big Owl nodded. "That is good. It is said that if you dream about a horse you have never seen, it is because the Great One wants you to have that horse."

"Where will I find him?" Claw Foot leaned forward anxiously.

"I cannot say," answered Big Owl. "Perhaps

16

when you have come to manhood and join the braves who hunt the wild horses on the plains, you will find him."

"But that will be too late!" cried Claw Foot. "I want him soon. I want to go into manhood with my new name!"

"You are impatient," said Big Owl.

"Is there no other way?" asked Claw Foot quietly, ashamed of his outburst.

Big Owl was thoughtful. "In a few suns," he replied, "when our scouts find a wild herd, the braves will hunt the wild horses and will bring them into our camp corral. Perhaps your horse will be among those the braves bring."

"Then I may not need to wait long," Claw Foot said hopefully.

"There is greatness in patience," said Big Owl. "You promise me patience?"

Claw Foot trembled slightly. Patience was not easy for him. He would rather ride with the men. He would even ride behind the men and help bring the horses in, rather than wait patiently at the camp. But he knew that the men would not ask a boy with a twisted foot to ride with them. Even though Claw Foot was a good rider, he knew that the men thought he might be thrown from his horse during the hunt. If he were thrown, his lame foot would not let him get out of the way of danger fast enough.

Claw Foot finally answered Big Owl's question. "I promise you patience," he said quietly.

Claw Foot left the tepee of Big Owl and slowly made his way to the tepee of his father, Hurries-to-War. All day he dabbled with the paints for the design on his buffalo-hide shield—the shield that Hurries-to-War had made for the day when Claw Foot would be a man. But his thoughts were of horses, running wild and free, and he yearned for the horse that would be his very own. He could not help thinking about the horse with four white feet and wondering if such a horse would be brought in.

The howling signal calls of coyotes in the distance told of the night approaching. Soon the deep of the night closed in. The campfires were already lit, and there was singing and dancing. The women and children and the old men sang to bring the good spirits for the braves who would hunt horses. Claw Foot sang too. He sang for a horse with four white feet.

The next morning there was great excitement in

the camp. Claw Foot rushed outside. Red Duck was racing by. He reined in his horse and looked down at Claw Foot.

"The scouts have found a wild herd," he said. "The men are riding out to get them. My father says I can go at the rear of the band. White Feather goes too."

Then, hitting his horse with a willow switch, he galloped away.

Claw Foot's shoulders slumped. His mind was full of rebellious thoughts. Red Duck, who beat horses, could go on the hunt. White Feather, who was younger than he, could go on the hunt.

"Why must I always be left behind?" he thought in anguish.

Loneliness and sadness filled Claw Foot. Was he, after all, doomed forever to sit in a tepee with paints?

"No!" he cried aloud. "I will ride too!"

He half ran, half walked to the meadow where his father's horses were hobbled. His father had taken the fast brown horse. But the white-spotted pinto was there. Freeing her, Claw Foot jumped on her back and pressed his heels into her sides. He rode as fast as he could to the top of the hill. There he would get a view of the men. He would catch up and follow in the rear with Red Duck and White Feather.

From the top of the hill Claw Foot could see clouds of dust. There they were! He could catch up!

He was just about to urge his pinto on, when in his mind he heard the voice of Big Owl saying, "You promise me patience?" And Claw Foot remembered his reply, "I promise you patience."

Wearily, Claw Foot turned his horse around and returned to camp.

The day was long. The laughter of the women and children filled the air. But as Claw Foot painted the designs of his people on his shield, his ears went beyond the laughter. He was listening for hoof-beats.

Finally, as the sun dipped near the edge of the sky, he heard them. The men were bringing the horses into the brush corral near the clump of trees by the brook.

Rushing to the corral, Claw Foot saw Big Owl leading a herd of horses. He was calling commands to the men who rode on either side of the herd.

Claw Foot could see that the horses were weary from the chase. He hurried closer to the corral. The

horses, still frightened, were milling about nervously. Claw Foot thought that his horse must be among these moving, whinnying horses. His eyes searched through the fast-falling darkness for a horse with white feet. But he could not see among the hundreds of stamping hooves.

"Lame one looks for a horse," laughed Red Duck as he rode by, straight and tall on his horse. "There might be a lame old mare for you."

Claw Foot clenched his fists and watched Red Duck ride off. Then he heard Big Owl's voice above him.

"Do not stay by the corral," commanded Big Owl. "The horses must have the night for quietness. They have had a hard day."

"But . . . but . . . ," stammered Claw Foot. "My horse . . ."

"Tomorrow we will come to the corral together," said Big Owl.

3
shadow

When the rising sun lightened the blue sky, Claw Foot jumped up and ran from the tepee, not bothering to stop by the stewpot. He was sure that Big Owl would be awake and ready to go to the corral.

At Big Owl's tepee he raised the flap and entered. The warrior lay in deep slumber on his robe.

"Big Owl," Claw Foot spoke softly.

The man stirred fitfully and frowned.

"I will not awaken him now. He might become angry," Claw Foot thought, and turned back.

Quickly he headed toward the corral, forgetting his promise of patience to Big Owl in his hurry to see the horses. Would the horse with four white feet be there? he wondered. His heart pounded as he came closer to the corral.

The horses were calm as his eyes searched among them. But Claw Foot knew they were aware of him by the way their ears shot forward when he came near. Grasping the top rail of the corral, he pulled himself up and sat on the rail. From there he could see better. He searched, his eyes darting rapidly back and forth from one horse to another. Was his horse in the herd? Or must he wait still longer for the horse he had seen in his dream?

And then, he saw him. In the corner of the corral stood a handsome creature, gray like the gray sky before the sun begins its journey. And his feet were white! All four feet were white!

Claw Foot shouted with the excitement of his find. "You are my horse!" he cried out.

Then, fearing he had frightened the horses too much, he slid quietly from the rail and cautiously approached his horse.

The horse bolted away with the others, his eyes widening. He turned to look back.

Claw Foot spoke through the distance between them. "I shall call you Shadow. You are the color of a shadow, and you were a shadow in my dream."

Shadow's left foot pawed the earth, and Claw Foot saw the white of his eyes. The horse's ears perked forward.

"You are my horse," Claw Foot told Shadow. "You and I will go many places together and do great deeds, and I shall be given a new name."

A laugh behind him made Claw Foot wheel in surprise. It was Red Duck.

"You who cannot even shoot an arrow through the hoop should not have such a fine horse. He would be wasted with such a rider," Red Duck said.

Claw Foot clenched his fists in anger.

"Shadow is mine!" he shouted at Red Duck. "I shall train him, and I shall know him and he shall know me!"

Claw Foot ran to the corral gate, opened it just enough to squeeze through, and made his way back to the tepee. He took down the buffalo-hair lasso that his father always kept on the tepee pole.

Claw Foot spoke aloud, "Shadow is mine. I shall train him."

Falling Star raised her eyes and was about to speak to him, but Claw Foot did not wait to hear. Red Duck's words were still strong in his ears. Besides, he knew he must hurry. He knew that a member of the tribe could have a captured horse only if he could train it. The first one to get the lasso over the horse's neck would be the owner.

Claw Foot ran back to the corral. He would start training Shadow now. There would be no doubt about whose horse he was.

As he approached the corral, he saw the horses milling and circling at the far end. Only one horse was at the end nearest the gate. It was Shadow. In the brightness of the day, he saw clearly that Shadow had a lasso around his neck and that he was tethered to a nearby tree.

As Claw Foot drew closer he saw Red Duck. In his hand Red Duck had a lance. He hurled it at Shadow's right leg.

Shadow reared and neighed. Blood spurted from his right front fetlock and dyed the hair crimson. His eyes rolled white, and his muscles tightened with pain.

"Red Duck!" yelled Claw Foot. "Stop! Stop!"

Red Duck turned, the lance poised high for

another strike at the agonized horse's foot.

"You can't stop me!" Red Duck shouted. He turned his back to Claw Foot and prepared to throw the lance.

Claw Foot wanted to jump on Red Duck and wrestle him to the ground. But he knew he was no match for Red Duck. Somehow he had to save Shadow from Red Duck's cruelty.

Grabbing the buffalo-hair lasso, he spun it high above his head and with careful aim threw it toward Red Duck. It hit the mark! The lasso fell neatly over Red Duck's shoulders just as he hurled the lance. The lance sailed unsteadily, missed its mark, and hit the ground. Shadow reared and his forefeet pawed the air.

Pulling the lasso with all his strength, Claw Foot dragged Red Duck toward him. Red Duck pulled back. He squirmed and twisted one way and then the other. He strained against the lasso until the veins in his neck stood out in his skin like snakes.

Claw Foot pulled the lasso tighter and tighter. Then he jerked it suddenly. Red Duck stumbled and fell to the ground with a thump. Gathering in the lasso, Claw Foot came close to the still-writhing Red Duck.

"Why do you want to hurt my horse?" Claw Foot
shouted, his eyes piercing Red Duck like arrows.

"A crippled brave should have a crippled horse,"
Red Duck shouted back defiantly.

"You will never touch my horse again," Claw

Foot said. He clenched his fist menacingly as Red Duck struggled to his feet.

"Loosen the lasso," someone called from the corral gate. It was Big Owl.

Claw Foot let the lasso drop from his hands. Red Duck, freed of his bonds, stood straight, with legs astride as if to brace himself for whatever would happen next.

Big Owl scowled. His face looked like the face of a man who approaches an enemy.

"Go!" he commanded Red Duck. "You have proven to me that you are not ready for the test of manhood."

Red Duck's shoulders slumped as he left the corral. Claw Foot knew that Red Duck's punishment was worse than anything Claw Foot could have done to him.

"Did you not promise me patience? Did I not say we would come to the corral together?" Claw Foot heard Big Owl ask. "Red Duck would not have hurt the horse if I had been here."

Claw Foot felt too ashamed to meet Big Owl's gaze. He hung his head and repeated Big Owl's words sadly. "If I had kept my promise and waited patiently for you, my horse would not be hurt."

"You acted wisely and well to protect the horse upon which you brought so much pain," Big Owl said in consoling tones. "But he is not your horse or anyone else's horse yet."

"Red Duck threw the lasso . . ." Claw Foot wanted to put the question of ownership to Big Owl, but he was too ashamed to continue.

"If a horse cannot walk, he is of no use," Big Owl said.

"If I make his foot well . . ." Claw Foot tried again to ask the important question.

Big Owl said, "Red Duck's lasso was thrown for harm. Throw a lasso out of kindness. If you can make the horse's foot of use again, you may try to train him and make him your own."

Big Owl turned and walked away.

4
TO RIDE A HORSE

Claw Foot looked back at Shadow. The gray horse stood alone. His head hung low, and his injured foot was raised slightly off the ground.

"I will get good medicine for your leg," Claw Foot called to the horse. As he hurried back to the tepee, White Feather came to meet him.

"Red Duck has been in the tepee of his father for a very long time. What has happened?" White Feather asked.

As the boys walked along, Claw Foot told his friend about Shadow. He told him about Red

31

Duck's attack on Shadow and about Big Owl's wise words.

"I must get good medicine for Shadow," he said.

"I will help you, my friend," White Feather promised.

At the tepee, Falling Star sat on the ground. Her hands were idle.

"Why are you not working?" Claw Foot asked.

"The braves do not find buffalo. I have no work to do," she answered. Worry lines deepened across her forehead.

"They will find buffalo," Claw Foot said confidently. "Do we have root medicine?"

Falling Star nodded toward a buffalo-skin bucket near the tepee. Claw Foot grabbed it and told White Feather to pick up the empty bucket nearby.

"You get water from the creek and meet me at the corral," Claw Foot said. "I will try to put the noose over Shadow's neck. When you come back, we'll mix good medicine in the water and wash his wounds."

At the corral Claw Foot had no trouble finding Shadow. The gray horse stood all alone. His whole body looked weary, and his head drooped.

"Do not be afraid of me, Shadow," Claw Foot

said as he stole nearer the horse. He fingered part of his lasso. "Don't fight me. I want to help you."

He walked closer to the horse. Shadow's head came up and his eyes grew wild. Quick as lightning, he bolted into the rest of the herd.

White Feather joined Claw Foot at the end of the corral. They both stared hopelessly at the milling horses.

"He will not get better if I do not help him," Claw Foot told his friend. "And I cannot help him if I cannot catch him."

"You cannot catch him," said White Feather. "He is too wild and too smart to be caught."

"I will try," said Claw Foot. He left the corral and limped with as long a stride as he could toward the pasture where his father's bay horse was tethered.

It was not long before Claw Foot was back at the corral astride his father's horse. White Feather opened the corral gate for him. Claw Foot rode toward the excited horses and around the outer part of the milling herd. He searched for the only horse who was the color of the sky at the beginning of the day. Then at the far side of the corral he saw Shadow standing motionless and limp.

He rode his horse as close to Shadow as he

dared. With several deft twirls, he threw the lasso. Quickly it slipped over Shadow's ears. Shadow shook and tried to rear. Claw Foot dismounted and came closer to Shadow. The horse's sides heaved as Claw Foot pulled the noose tight.

"Now," said Claw Foot to White Feather. "Now we give him the medicine."

White Feather hurried to bring the biggest buffalo-hide bucket. Claw Foot added the medicine from the small bucket.

"Hold the noose," he commanded White Feather.

Cautiously he lifted the suffering horse's leg. He felt a quiver run through Shadow's body as he placed the injured leg in the bucket. Claw Foot put his hands in the bucket and stroked gently down the leg, splashing medicine water over the wounds.

Shadow's breathing was fast. His eyes showed white. His tail twitched. He strained to get loose, but the noose held him fast.

Claw Foot continued bathing the injured leg, speaking softly as he worked.

"I will come again and again to bathe you with good medicine. You will walk straight and sure. We will ride together. We will earn my new name," he said.

White Feather slackened the noose and Claw Foot reached to take it off.

As the two boys walked toward the circle of tepees, Claw Foot asked, "Will you return to the corral with me every day when the sun rises and when the sun goes over the edge of the world?"

"Yes," nodded White Feather.

When Claw Foot entered the corral each day, he gave a bird-song whistle. He always heard an answering snort. The noose was thrown around Shadow's neck, and his foot was placed in the buffalo-hide bucket. Gradually the beautiful horse grew calmer. Each day he resisted the noose less.

On the fourth day, when Claw Foot and White Feather entered the corral, Claw Foot whistled. He heard the familiar snort. Shadow, as if waiting for him, trotted along the fence.

"Today," he told White Feather, "I shall ride Shadow. I'll begin by riding my father's horse around the corral. Then I'll slip the noose over Shadow's ears and jump on his back. You must be ready to ride my father's horse away."

White Feather nodded that he understood. But his eyes showed fear.

"He could kill you," he said.

35

"He will not fight me," Claw Foot said over his shoulder. "He knows I am his friend. Did I not heal his leg?"

He rode close to Shadow. He threw his lasso and tightened the noose. Then he jumped from the bay mare and sat squarely on Shadow's back.

At the same time a great tremor ran through his mount. Shadow lifted his head high. Claw Foot grabbed for the thick mane. Then he felt himself being lifted through the air. He hit the ground with a shaking jolt.

White Feather hurried to help him.

"Do not try," he pleaded. "He will hurt you. He's a wild one."

"He is not mine until I ride him," Claw Foot gasped.

His foot throbbed with pain and he felt soreness down into his bones. But he mounted his father's bay once again.

Once again he jumped on Shadow's back. Again Shadow trembled, threw his head, and kicked with wild abandon. For the second time Claw Foot felt himself lifted through the air. He hit the ground with a thud, and his head reeled. Red, green, and blue flashed before his eyes.

36

"He's a wild one," White Feather said, helping Claw Foot to his feet. The two boys stood and watched Shadow gallop to the far end of the corral.

"I think I know how he moves now," Claw Foot said. "He will not throw me too easily this time."

"Not again," White Feather protested. "You will not take another fall today!"

"Now," said Claw Foot. He saw fear in White Feather's eyes, but he saw admiration too.

He shook his head as if to clear it and then mounted the bay. Singling out Shadow from among the excited horses, he threw the lasso, pulled the struggling horse to a halt, and jumped.

As soon as he mounted Shadow, the tremor went through the horse. He veered this way and that. Suddenly he reared up and pawed the air with his front legs. But Claw Foot was ready for him this time. He dug his hands into the mane and grasped the horse's sides with his heels.

Shadow reared again, his forefeet pawing. Claw Foot moved with Shadow's every movement. He made himself feel as if he were part of the horse.

After a few more moments of rearing and snorting, Shadow satisfied himself with trotting into the middle of the excited herd.

Then, as he approached the gate end of the corral, Claw Foot called out to White Feather, "Open the gate!"

Shadow ran. It was a steady, rapid, pulsing run. The wind whizzed by and bathed Claw Foot's face. Claw Foot was happy as he felt the sure-footed strength beneath him.

Claw Foot thought, "He is strong. He has four good feet. He will give me his strength and his sure-footedness to find a new name."

At the meadow, where the grass was thickest, Claw Foot slowed Shadow to a stop.

Shadow stood calmly, sweaty and tired, his big heart bumping against his side. He tossed his gray mane and turned his face toward Claw Foot.

Claw Foot stood close as Shadow grazed and drank at the stream. Together they smelled the clean air and listened to the soft sounds of living things.

"Tomorrow," said Claw Foot, "we ride to do great deeds. Tomorrow we look for a new name."

5
THE SEARCH

The next morning, when the sun was beginning its climb into the sky, Claw Foot was awakened by voices outside the tepee.

He heard his father say, "We go out again today. Today we must go farther to find buffalo. If we find them, be ready to move from this camp. We must follow the buffalo."

As his mother spoke, she sounded worried. "Many are hungry. There will be sickness and death if we do not find buffalo," she said.

Claw Foot listened intently, staring wide-eyed in the direction of the voices. He remembered that yesterday the stewpot had been empty, and that he had eaten only berries and some dried meat that White Feather had given him. He remembered that his mother had told him she had no work because there were no buffalo, and that the braves could not find buffalo. His thoughts had not been on food. He had been thinking only of Shadow, of Shadow's sore leg, and of making Shadow his own horse.

New thoughts of the hunger that faced his people sent him springing to his feet.

He went to his father and mother. "I want to go with you!" he told Hurries-to-War.

"You have not yet come to manhood," said his father, shaking his head sadly. "You must remain here." With these words Hurries-to-War mounted his horse and rode through the village to join the other braves who were already gathered.

Claw Foot stood by his mother for a moment, gazing across the wide plains. The long summer day was just beginning. It was rising dry and hot.

"Lately I do not think of my people," Claw Foot told Falling Star. "I think only of my name. My new name should be Selfish One. And that is not even as good a name as Claw Foot."

41

Falling Star looked at him. "To serve your people well is more important than to have a great name," she said.

Claw Foot tried hard to swallow the choking lump in his throat. "How could I forget my people?" he thought.

Unhappiness lay on Claw Foot like the dirt of a dusty trail. He set out walking. As he rounded the circle of tepees, he saw old people sitting in the sun. Women and children were carrying buckets toward the thickets where there were berries. There was no laughter. There was no smoke from the stewpots. As he passed the tepee of Big Owl, he yearned to talk to him. But Big Owl, like all the braves, was scouting for buffalo.

Suddenly Claw Foot paused. Now that he had a horse, he could ride where the buffalo scouts had not ridden. He too could search for buffalo to feed his people!

He spun around and hurried back to the tepee. Falling Star was just returning with water from the stream. She looked at him in wonder.

"What makes you so happy?" she asked.

"I am going to scout the buffalo," Claw Foot said, smiling.

"But your father . . . ," Falling Star reminded him.

"I know I have not yet come to manhood," Claw Foot interrupted, "but you said that to serve my people is more important than to have a great name. Then, to serve my people is also more important than waiting to come to manhood. Is it not better to help when their need is great? Is it not better to search for buffalo than to sit here like an old woman and wait for my people to die of starvation?"

Falling Star sank down in the shade. No words came to her lips.

Finally she spoke. "You want to scout buffalo alone?" she asked. Her voice was calm. Still, it was heavy with worry.

But Claw Foot felt he could almost read Falling Star's thoughts. She was thinking that since he now had a horse of his own and was an able rider, he might cover ground that the men had not yet been able to cover. Perhaps she was thinking that a single horse could go unseen by an enemy where many horses could not.

Claw Foot trembled with excitement.

"Shadow is a strong horse. He has four sure feet.

He is brave, and he knows me as I know him," Claw Foot told his mother. "He will carry me well."

"Do not go too far north," said Falling Star, giving her consent without saying so. "The Crow, our enemies, are to the north. Our scouts do not go north."

Claw Foot stiffened. "If our scouts do not go north, and they have found no buffalo to the east, west, or south . . . buffalo must be north!" he cried.

"The Crow are a cruel enemy," warned Falling Star.

Claw Foot smiled to show his mother he was not afraid. Scouting buffalo would be a greater adventure than he had ever planned. Only yesterday he had thought of nothing but a new name. Today, the needs of his people were more important.

Falling Star handed him a pouch of pemmican, the buffalo meat he had seen her pound and mix with wild cherries.

"There is not much food," she said.

Reaching for his bow and arrows, he turned toward the meadow. As he walked along he kicked at pebbles with his gnarled foot. It was the only way he knew to let out his doubts and fears without showing weakness.

At the pasture he whistled and heard the answering whinny. He saw Shadow wheel. The horse snorted at Claw Foot's approach and backed away.

Claw Foot drew close. Cautiously he swung himself on Shadow's back. He felt the gray horse's body tremble. He saw the ears perk forward. Shadow's left hoof pawed the earth three times, but he made no effort to rear. Claw Foot knew that he and Shadow were ready to ride.

The sun was climbing high when Claw Foot headed north. The landscape lay rocky and quiet before him.

When he had gone some distance from his village, he scanned the countryside for a sign of buffalo. He was aware of every snake that crawled nearby, of every bird that circled the sky. He thought he saw and heard everything around him. Still, he had the uneasy feeling that eyes were watching him. Something was in the air, something soundless and strange.

As the sun dipped over the edge of the world, Claw Foot came to a place where big rocks lay on patches of grassy land. The grass was limp and sticky with dust. But a stream trickled by.

"We will make camp here," Claw Foot told

Shadow, as he scanned the place carefully. "We are safe here."

He tethered his horse near the stream where the grass was thickest, ate sparingly of the pemmican, and lay down close behind a boulder. Soon he closed his eyes to uneasy sleep. He dreamed of standing by a campfire, telling of his great deeds. He dreamed of the council giving him a new name.

At the beginning of daylight, Claw Foot rubbed the sleep from his eyes and looked around. He gasped with surprise. Shadow was gone! His bow and arrows were gone! He groped on the ground for the pouch of pemmican. It was gone too! He whirled frantically in search of a sign. Where was the enemy? Who had taken his horse, his weapon, his food? Fear caused great dizziness in his head.

Standing motionless, he put his tongue between his teeth and gave out a loud bird-whistle. There was no answering whinny.

Claw Foot turned his face toward the sky and cried out in desperation. "Great One," he shouted, "why do you desert me? Why do you desert me when my people face starvation?"

After his outcry, Claw Foot felt calmer. He tried to think about what he must do.

He looked again at his unfamiliar surroundings. Somewhere out there was a thief who had robbed him of all he had. If the thief was a Crow, why had he not killed him?

Claw Foot blinked in the bright sunshine. He had to find Shadow. Perhaps he could find the Crow village under the cover of night and take Shadow back. It was good at least that his knife was still hidden in his belt. Now it was all he had.

Claw Foot continued his journey to the north on foot. He hurried over rocks that bruised and cut him. His gnarled foot scuffed along, raising puffs of dust where the grass was thin.

Claw Foot walked on and on. He walked all day. He slept briefly when darkness came, and wakened at the first glow of the sun. He walked until the sun made its circle in the sky three times, pausing sometimes to whistle and to wait for the answering whinny that never came. Thirst parched his throat. He was very hungry. His hunger was like a snake, coiling and biting in his stomach. The strength was leaving his legs.

Finally, when he knew he could go no farther, he spotted a half-hidden stream winding around a clump of cottonwoods. Lying flat on his stomach,

47

Claw Foot dropped his face to the water and drank.
Then he rolled over and stretched himself on the
stream's rocky bed.

The water moved gently over his body. It soothed
the pains in his legs. He lay there a long time,
reluctant to leave the goodness of the water.

Finally, he forced himself to rise and to continue walking to the north.

Often during his journey, he sat on rocks to rest. At these times he wondered if he would see buffalo, and if he did, how he could get word to his people. Would he ever see Shadow again? Would he ever see his mother and father and White Feather and Big Owl?

Weakness was in him like a sickness. He gritted his teeth and walked on. As he walked he looked up at the darkening sky. Black clouds roamed as restlessly as corralled horses. Thunder sounded as though the rocks in the hills were splitting away from the earth.

He climbed a slope where he thought he could find shelter from the coming storm. Halfway up, he stopped and caught his breath in surprise.

There, surrounded by a tangle of wild shrubs, was the dark opening of a rocky cave. Nearby, tethered to a tree stump, stood Shadow!

6
AN UNEXPECTED MEETING

"Shadow!" called Claw Foot, his heart leaping with joy.

Half running, half stumbling up the slope, Claw Foot paid no attention to the jagged rocks, or to the thorny weeds that scratched his skin. He saw only Shadow.

As he came near Shadow, he saw that the great gray horse was covered with lather. Eagerly Claw Foot leaned forward and slid his hand along Shadow's wet neck.

"You have been running too hard," he said close

to Shadow's ear. "Now that I have found you, you will not be treated this way again."

Shadow nuzzled Claw Foot with his proud head. In the gathering storm there was joy between them.

Claw Foot started to untie the rope that held Shadow to the stump. When he looked up, there stood Red Duck!

"You!" Claw Foot gasped. "What are you . . ."

Red Duck stood facing Claw Foot with narrowed eyes. "You left camp to win glory," he said. "I followed. A crippled one should not win honor. I, Red Duck, will be a great warrior. I am the one who will find buffalo and be talked about beside many campfires."

Lightning flashed across the sky, and thunder warned of the approaching storm. Claw Foot felt a storm inside his body, too. He braced himself to leap at Red Duck. It did not matter to him that he could not win in a fight with Red Duck. He wanted only to strike him.

Suddenly the rain came—a hard rain that pelted Claw Foot's body and face so that he could hardly see. Struggling through the downpour, Claw Foot groped toward Shadow. He untied the horse and led him under the shelter of the overhanging rocks

51

at the cave's entrance. Now he saw that two other horses were already tethered there.

The cave was a small, hollowed-out space in the side of the slope, protected by a roof of rock. Inside, a tiny fire was smoldering on the ground, and shadows jumped and flickered on the rocky walls. In the dim light stood Red Duck. Next to him was someone else. It was White Feather!

White Feather spoke. "I followed Red Duck when I saw him follow you. I want to help you."

"You will be in trouble, White Feather," said Claw Foot. "He will, too." He pointed to Red Duck. "I had the right to leave, given me by my mother."

"I will not get in trouble," said Red Duck. "Not when I tell them I left to follow you."

Claw Foot turned from him. "Why," he asked himself, "must there always be Red Duck?"

Then he noticed that near the fire lay three pemmican pouches. Suddenly, even Red Duck seemed unimportant in comparison with the sharp pains in Claw Foot's stomach. The sight of food made him wild with hunger.

Claw Foot pulled out his knife. Red Duck muttered a threat and, with arms braced for defense, took several steps toward him.

Claw Foot waved him away. Knife in hand, he moved forward until he reached the fire. He quickly pulled open one pouch, cut a chunk of pemmican, and devoured it without even stopping to chew. White Feather and Red Duck watched silently as Claw Foot ate piece after piece of pemmican, until he could eat no more.

When his hunger was finally satisfied, weariness came over Claw Foot, and he sank down beside the fire.

"We stay here until it is light," Red Duck told him. "Then we go back."

"Yes," said White Feather. "We have seen a small herd grazing not far away. We will tell our braves where to hunt for buffalo."

"Buffalo!" exclaimed Claw Foot happily. "The Great One will not let our people starve!"

The three boys stretched themselves out on the hard ground beside the fire. At least they were safe from the rain that pounded on the ground outside. Claw Foot was happy. There was food in his stomach, and Shadow was tethered safely. With buffalo sighted nearby, and his best friend to share all the good fortune, Claw Foot felt a calm he had not felt in many suns.

"Now that our people are saved from hunger," he thought, "surely now I will find a new name."

Claw Foot slept a deep, sound sleep. But toward dawn, he began to dream a strange and troubling dream, filled with violent confusion and the noise of whinnying horses. Suddenly he was wide awake. Rough hands twisted his arms. He turned quickly. Behind him were five Crow braves! They had entered the cave so silently that none of the boys had awakened until it was too late.

Now, two braves were shoving White Feather outside, and two others were wrestling with Red Duck. The fifth one glowered at Claw Foot as he made a horsehair rope secure around his hands. The two eagle feathers in his headband scratched Claw Foot's back as the Crow bent to fasten the rope tighter.

Claw Foot felt half-choked with fear. The rope cut into his flesh, and the Crow's rough hands bruised his skin. All his newfound feelings of hope and bravery disappeared.

Outside, the sun had begun its journey across the sky. Peaceful clouds showed no sign of the night's storm. The earth smelled fresh, and grasses dripped wet across Claw Foot's moccasins.

The Crow pushed the three of them toward the horses. What would the Crow do with them? Where would they take them?

Shadow's eyes were wide. His ears perked forward, and he danced nervously. The Crow threw a noose over Shadow's ears and led him with a rope.

"Do not fight the rope." Claw Foot spoke soothingly in his ear. "I do not want you beaten."

At the sound of Claw Foot's voice, Shadow quieted. All the riders mounted their horses. Three of the Crow held the lead ropes. The one with the two eagle feathers in his headband rode ahead to show the way.

A trail wound before them. The sun was high in the sky before the Crow stopped by a stream to rest and drink. Where were they going? Claw Foot wondered. He saw cruelty in the eyes of the silent Crow braves. He sensed the rising fears of White Feather and Red Duck.

At last, Claw Foot looked down from the bluff and saw a valley. There was a circle of tepees near a tumbling stream. Thin streaks of smoke were rising from the tepee cones. It looked peaceful and safe. But Claw Foot knew there was no safety for a Sioux in a Crow village.

7
bROKEN WiNG

In front of a tepee decorated with many paint-
ings, the Crow braves made a sign for their captives
to dismount. Claw Foot slid from Shadow's back.
He saw firelight flickering behind the flap of the
tepee and smelled the strong odor of food.

His captor pushed him into the tepee, and White
Feather and Red Duck stumbled in beside him.
The chief of the Crow sat cross-legged on a robe not
far from the fire. He had broad shoulders. His face
looked as if it were carved from the rock of the
ridges that surrounded the village. The Crow with
the two eagle feathers spoke, but Claw Foot did
not understand his language.

The chief looked from one to the other. There was a grim, set look on his face. He looked hard and straight into Claw Foot's eyes.

Claw Foot tried to stand erect. He knew that the Crow, like the Sioux, hated a show of weakness. There was a long silence. The chief studied Claw Foot's gnarled foot, which even Falling Star's carefully made moccasin could not disguise. As the chief stared, his right hand went awkwardly to his left arm. Claw Foot saw that the chief's left arm was twisted and bent to uselessness.

The chief spoke, addressing himself to Claw Foot. "I know your language," he said. "What are you called?"

"I am Claw Foot," Claw Foot answered, even though he hated saying his name.

"I am Broken Wing," the chief said. "It was not always so. On a buffalo hunt, many moons ago . . ." The chief did not finish. His eyes were sad.

"Why do you come to the land of the Crow?" Broken Wing asked.

Claw Foot still felt afraid, but he knew this was his chance to save himself and the others. If he could stir the sympathy that he sensed behind that rigid face, perhaps the Crow would not harm them.

58

Claw Foot swallowed hard. Then he spoke. "My people are near starvation. Our herds are gone. Our braves have traveled many moons to find buffalo," Claw Foot told the chief.

"You were brave but foolish to come to our land," Broken Wing said.

"I want to help my people!" Claw Foot exclaimed frantically. "My foot, my name . . . they are not important. My people may die!" He straightened his tired shoulders.

Broken Wing's eyes looked into his. A light flickered in them for an instant. Claw Foot felt a surge of hope. Broken Wing understood!

Claw Foot waited anxiously for Broken Wing's next words. Behind him, Red Duck's breathing was loud. He heard White Feather catch his breath between his teeth.

Broken Wing finally spoke. "You put the need of your people above your own. My people, too, are more important than this useless arm," he said. "Claw Foot, I shall give you one buffalo that my hunters have killed. I shall let you and your friends go back to your people, but I will have your word that you will not come to Crow land again."

"But one buffalo will not last long." Claw Foot could not keep the pleading tone from his voice.

"One buffalo. Meat and hide," said Broken Wing. "Take your buffalo when the sun rises. Thank the Great One that the Crow did not kill you."

Suddenly, as Claw Foot thought about the uselessness of one buffalo for the many moons ahead, an idea came to him. It made his heart beat fast. He would try once more for his people.

"May I have the land that this one buffalo hide will cover?" he asked.

Broken Wing scowled. "That is a foolish request," he said. "One hide would not cover enough ground for one tepee."

"Perhaps I can stretch the hide," Claw Foot said.

Broken Wing frowned impatiently. He looked at Claw Foot's moccasin. Then his eyes studied Claw Foot's face with a look Claw Foot had seen before. He had seen it on his father's face many times. It was a look that said, "He is young and foolish, but he tries, and tries, and tries."

"You may have the land one hide covers," Broken Wing nodded.

"And I must have the freedom to ride over your land to find a place for my hide," Claw Foot said with new confidence.

At Broken Wing's hesitation, he added, "I will not try to escape. We will not do anything wrong. I give my word as a Sioux."

Broken Wing nodded, and the three captives were untied and led away by the brave with two eagle feathers. Claw Foot was pushed roughly into a tepee at the far side of the circle. A stewpot hung over a fire, and there were robes on which to sleep.

"What can we do with the land one hide covers?" scoffed Red Duck between gulps of food.

White Feather stopped eating, a strip of buffalo meat dripping in his fingers, and waited for Claw Foot's answer.

But Claw Foot did not want to disturb his thoughts by answering Red Duck. He needed to lay his plans carefully. He dipped into the buffalo stew and did not answer. His wrists were bruised and sore, but he gave them little thought. He thought of his plan.

His plan was clear when the sun came up over the edge of the world. He knew what he had to do. He found the part of the camp where the buffalo was skinned and the meat cut up in chunks. There he picked up the buffalo hide that Broken Wing had promised him. Claw Foot dragged the hide to the grassy spot where Shadow was tied. He slung the hide over the gray horse's shoulder and climbed on.

Shadow tossed his head and stamped a front hoof. Claw Foot dug his heels into Shadow's flanks and turned the horse's head to the south. Then, in a flash of movement, Shadow broke from a trot to a gallop.

Claw Foot rode beyond the ridges, far to the south. Only occasionally he stopped to gulp clear water from a stream and to rest Shadow. He saw signs of buffalo, and his heart sang.

Then, as Shadow trotted at an easy pace, Claw Foot drew out his knife, which was still hidden in his belt. He began cutting pieces of hide and throwing them on the ground.

He cut piece after piece, scattering them great distances apart. When he no longer had a single scrap of hide left, he turned Shadow toward the Crow village.

There was an orange sun going down over the edge of the world when Claw Foot approached the village. His pulse quickened at the thought that he would soon be facing Broken Wing again. Would Broken Wing keep his word?

Back at Broken Wing's tepee, he lifted the flap and entered. There, right before him, stood Big Owl! The Crow with two eagle feathers stood to one side. Broken Wing, who sat cross-legged before the fire, stopped talking when he saw Claw Foot.

"Big Owl!" Claw Foot cried.

There was a hint of reproach in Big Owl's eyes. "I am glad I found you," he said.

"Found me?" Claw Foot asked breathlessly.

"When I returned to our village after scouting for buffalo and you were gone—you and White Feather and Red Duck—Hurries-to-War agreed that I must find you," Big Owl explained. With that his captor pushed him and made a sign for him to be quiet.

"The Crow found me first," Big Owl added, ignoring the brave with two eagle feathers.

Claw Foot took another step forward. He talked to the chief. "Big Owl is my friend. You promised to let my friends go."

The chief hesitated. "Broken Wing keeps a promise," he finally said.

Claw Foot was relieved. Broken Wing's words gave him the courage to ask the question upon which so much depended.

He swallowed hard against the lump in his throat and said, "I have come for my land."

"What land?" asked Broken Wing.

"The land one buffalo hide covers," Claw Foot answered.

64

Broken Wing was thoughtful. He said, "My scouts tell me you cut the buffalo hide in many pieces and threw the pieces on the ground."

"The many pieces are spread over enough land for my people. Enough land to make a village and to hunt the buffalo," Claw Foot explained.

Big Owl shot him a quick glance of admiration.

Broken Wing looked up at Claw Foot and then at his moccasined feet. He said, "Only your body is lame, not your thoughts. You have outwitted me fairly. You may have the land."

Claw Foot thanked Broken Wing solemnly, hoping his voice did not show how much relief he felt. He looked up at Big Owl, but the warrior's head was bent in deep thought.

At last Big Owl raised his eyes and spoke to Claw Foot. "From this day on," he said, "you will not be known as Claw Foot. From this day on your name is He Who Thinks."

Claw Foot thought his chest would burst from holding back shouts of joy!

As he and Big Owl left the tepee, Claw Foot looked happily at the other two captives, who were standing just outside. He looked from one face to the other.

White Feather had a look of bewildered pleasure as he shouted, "Hoye!"

Red Duck turned toward Claw Foot awkwardly and hung his head to avoid Claw Foot's eyes.

"He Who Thinks, you are a leader among our people," he said. "One day you will be chief. I hope that I may be among your warriors."

"I am thankful for my new name," said He Who Thinks. "I shall try to keep it a strong name for the good of my people."

He turned and whistled to Shadow. And as he mounted the proud gray horse, he silently thanked the Great One for his good fortune. By serving his people, he had at last earned for himself a name befitting the son of a great chief. He Who Thinks knew that this was truly the most important day of his life.

About the Author

Evelyn Witter is a teacher, writer, and lecturer who has published a variety of books and magazine articles for children. After receiving her B.S. degree in education at the University of Illinois, Mrs. Witter went on to pursue a career as a history teacher. She now makes her home in Milan, Illinois, where she teaches, writes, and enjoys her hobby of antique collecting. In recent years, she has also been an active participant in writers' workshops and conferences throughout the Midwest.

BOOKS ABOUT THE
FIRST AMERICANS

NON-FICTION

The American Indian in America, Vol. I
Prehistory to the End of the 18th Century

The American Indian in America, Vol. II
Early 19th Century to the Present

Among the Plains Indians

The Collector's Guide to American Indian Artifacts

Indian Chiefs

Let Me Be a Free Man
A Documentary History of Indian Resistance

Patrick Des Jarlait
The Story of an American Indian Artist

The Red Man in Art

We Rode the Wind
Recollections of 19th Century Tribal Life

FICTION

Prisoner of the Mound Builders

Hunters of the Black Swamp

Claw Foot

LERNER PUBLICATIONS COMPANY
241 First Avenue North, Minneapolis, Minnesota 55401